STAR TREK

THE

TRIBBLE™
Handbook

TERRY J. ERDMANN

An *Original* Publication of POCKET BOOKS

POCKET BOOKS, a division of Simon & Schuster Inc.
1230 Avenue of the Americas, New York, NY 10020

Design by David Stevenson. Illustrations by Doug Drexler.

ISBN: 0-671-02748-4

First Pocket Books trade paperback printing December 1998

10 9 8 7 6 5 4 3

POCKET and colophon are registered trademarks of
Simon & Schuster Inc.

Printed in the U.S.A.

INTRODUCTION

*T*he most popular guest characters to appear in the original *Star Trek* series spoke no lines.

Small of stature and quite round in shape these life-forms made their lasting contribution to the Federation by eating, reproducing and, occasionally, by hissing at the nearest Klingon. Of all the beings ever encountered on the historic five-year mission, only this species managed to upstage the captain, and the entire Enterprise crew for that matter, by quietly being themselves.

We're talking about tribbles, of course.

Remember, they aren't just any furballs — they're tribbles, the most fabulous furballs in the galaxy!

WHAT WE DO KNOW ABOUT TRIBBLES

1. They're "the sweetest creatures known to man."[1]

2. They purr when they like people—and they seem to like everyone, with the exception of Klingons.[2]

3. They have no teeth.

4. Their trilling seems to have a tranquilizing effect on the human nervous system.[3]

5. Vulcans are immune to this effect.[4]

---

[1] According to Cyrano Jones. However, to be fair, if you're going to accept unscientific hearsay, then you can just as easily accept Worf's judgement that they are "detestable."

[2] Based upon their reaction to Odo, we must assume they have no inherent prejudice against changelings. However, we're not laying any odds when it comes to the Borg or the Jem'Hadar.

[3] It seems to have a similar effect on the nervous systems of changelings and Ferengi.

[4] Although not, apparently, half-Vulcans.

6. They are mature enough
to leave their parent
after one day.[5]

7. Almost fifty percent
of their metabolism
is geared
for reproduction.[6]

8. The more they eat,
the more they reproduce.
Conversely, if you stop
feeding them,
they stop breeding.

9. The good: they're nice,
   they're soft and
   furry, they make a
   pleasant sound,
they do not talk too much.

10. The bad: they have no
    practical use, they eat a
    great deal, they seem to
    be born pregnant.

11. They are "bisexual,"
    reproducing at will.

---

[5] Per Uhura. Not a scientific judgement, but she appears to have been correct.

[6] One can assume that the other fifty percent is geared for digestion.

12. They have "a lot of will."

13. They are "the only love money can buy."[7]

14. They originally developed in a predator-filled environment.

15. They are "not dangerous."[8]

16. They like chicken sandwiches and coffee.[9]

17. Under optimal conditions, the average tribble is capable of producing a litter of ten every twelve hours.

---

[7] More hearsay from Cyrano Jones, who, we are certain, also has a bridge to sell.

[8] Per Cyrano Jones. The definition of "dangerous" is, of course, relative.

[9] You'd probably be hard-pressed to find something edible that they don't like.

18. They are "very perceptive creatures."[10]

19. They were once considered mortal enemies of the Klingon Empire, considered "an ecological menace, a plague to be wiped out."[11]

20. Hundreds of Klingon warriors tracked them down throughout the galaxy, and an armada obliterated the tribble homeworld.[12]

21. By the end of the 23rd century, the species had been "eradicated."[13]

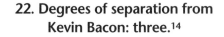

22. Degrees of separation from Kevin Bacon: three.[14]

---

[10] Per Spock, although this appears to be a very subjective evaluation.

[11] According to Worf. He did not indicate when this judgement was made, but it seems likely that it was after Scotty transported the *Enterprise*'s tribbles to the engine room of Koloth's ship.

[12] Again, all of these activities would seem to have commenced *after* Scotty transported the tribbles.

[13] Per Worf. Pretty nasty, but if it's any consolation, it could be propoganda, since no one in the Federation seems to have heard about this.

[14] Take your choice: Bacon was in 1979's *Starting Over* with Wallace Shawn, who has frequently guested on *Star Trek: Deep Space Nine*; he was also in 1988's *She's Having a Baby*, with William Windom, who guest-starred in the original series *Star Trek* episode "The Doomsday Machine."

WHAT WE DON'T KNOW ABOUT TRIBBLES

1. Prior to arriving at Deep Space Station K-7, how did Cyrano Jones keep his tribble population in check?

2. How long can a tribble survive without eating?

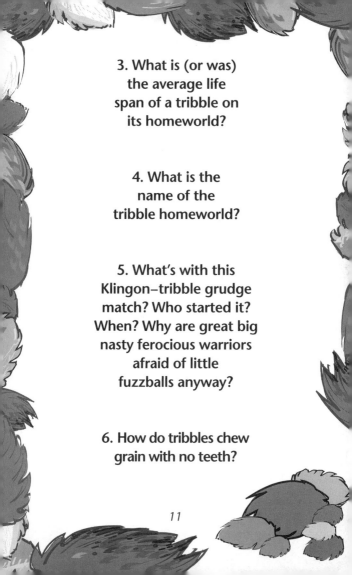

3. What is (or was) the average life span of a tribble on its homeworld?

4. What is the name of the tribble homeworld?

5. What's with this Klingon–tribble grudge match? Who started it? When? Why are great big nasty ferocious warriors afraid of little fuzzballs anyway?

6. How do tribbles chew grain with no teeth?

7. How do tribbles dispose of "waste matter"? Are they as messy as hamsters, or do they absorb every bit of nutrition from every morsel they ingest? If reproduction is tied into nutritional input, is it also connected to output?

8. Which end is the head on?

9. Do tribbles have feet? If not, how do they walk?

10. How do they stick to walls?

11. What does a naked tribble look like?

12. What happened to the tribbles in Koloth's engine room?

13. What happened to the tribbles on Deep Space 9?

14. If a tribble fought a Cardassian vole, who would win?

WHAT WE SORT OF KNOW ABOUT TRIBBLES

THE MISSING CHAPTER:

"MORE TRIBBLES, MORE TROUBLES"

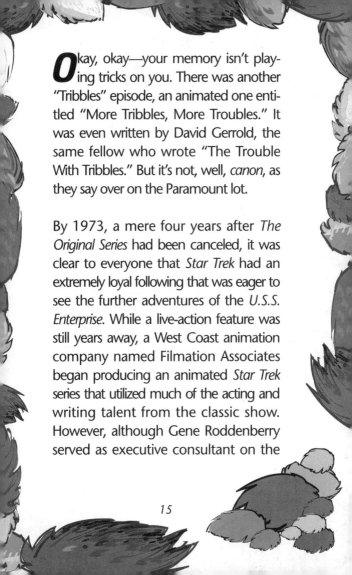

Okay, okay—your memory isn't playing tricks on you. There was another "Tribbles" episode, an animated one entitled "More Tribbles, More Troubles." It was even written by David Gerrold, the same fellow who wrote "The Trouble With Tribbles." But it's not, well, *canon*, as they say over on the Paramount lot.

By 1973, a mere four years after *The Original Series* had been canceled, it was clear to everyone that *Star Trek* had an extremely loyal following that was eager to see the further adventures of the *U.S.S. Enterprise*. While a live-action feature was still years away, a West Coast animation company named Filmation Associates began producing an animated *Star Trek* series that utilized much of the acting and writing talent from the classic show. However, although Gene Roddenberry served as executive consultant on the show, there were reportedly some aspects of the production with which he was never entirely happy. For that reason, the animated episodes are not considered "official."

However, since we know that anyone reading this book must be a tribble "completist" of the first order, here are a few more details about the little furballs that were established in that episode. Be warned, however—there are a few apparent contradictions, no doubt due to some predestination paradox. (We hate those.)

1. Although Spock had projected that it would take Cyrano Jones some seventeen years to get all of the tribbles off Deep Space Station K-7, Jones took a shortcut by bringing in a partner: a tribble predator called a *glommer*, which apparently

ate a large percentage of the
station's tribble population.[15]

**2. The glommer was a Klingon genetic
construct, developed by the Klingons
to help them eradicate some
tribbles that Jones sold
on a Klingon planet.[16]**

---

[15] Speculation.

[16] There's a bit of circular logic here. Jones admits that
he got the glommer from the Klingons, yet the
Klingons claim that they created the glommer to
help them deal with the tribbles that Jones sold
them. Exactly when Jones escaped from K-7 to sell
some tribbles to the Klingons—an impressive feat
considering the way tribbles and Klingons feel
about each other—is unclear. And he apparently
escaped a second time to return to the same planet
to pick up the glommer, which did not exist the
first time he visited the planet.

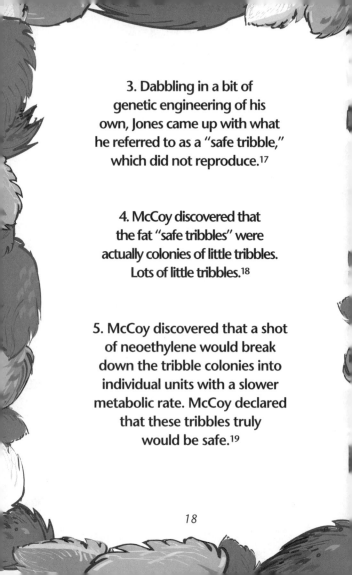

3. Dabbling in a bit of genetic engineering of his own, Jones came up with what he referred to as a "safe tribble," which did not reproduce.[17]

4. McCoy discovered that the fat "safe tribbles" were actually colonies of little tribbles. Lots of little tribbles.[18]

5. McCoy discovered that a shot of neoethylene would break down the tribble colonies into individual units with a slower metabolic rate. McCoy declared that these tribbles truly would be safe.[19]

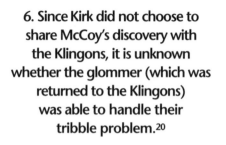

6. Since Kirk did not choose to share McCoy's discovery with the Klingons, it is unknown whether the glommer (which was returned to the Klingons) was able to handle their tribble problem.[20]

---

[17] What it does instead is get fat. Really fat. It is unknown whether the nauseatingly pink color of all the tribbles in this episode is also due to Jones' genetic tinkering.

[18] Due to the fact that Jones had managed to stop their reproduction but not their metabolism.

[19] We are inclined to stick with Spock's opinion earlier in the episode that a "safe tribble" is a contradiction in terms.

[20] One assumes not, in light of the subsequent massacre on the tribble homeworld (see "Trials and Tribble-ations").

DOES YOUR TRIBBLE HAVE A PEDIGREE?

"*T*o my best knowledge, there are only a couple of the original tribbles from 'The Trouble With Tribbles' left," says John Dwyer, set decorator for two of the three seasons of the original *Star Trek*. "But if you see one at a convention and the dealer claims

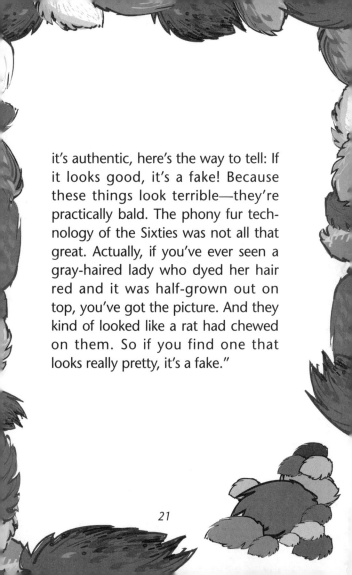

it's authentic, here's the way to tell: If it looks good, it's a fake! Because these things look terrible—they're practically bald. The phony fur technology of the Sixties was not all that great. Actually, if you've ever seen a gray-haired lady who dyed her hair red and it was half-grown out on top, you've got the picture. And they kind of looked like a rat had chewed on them. So if you find one that looks really pretty, it's a fake."

21

TWELVE GREAT J⬤KES THAT HAVEN'T BEEN WRITTEN ...YET

(Go ahead—knock yourself out!)

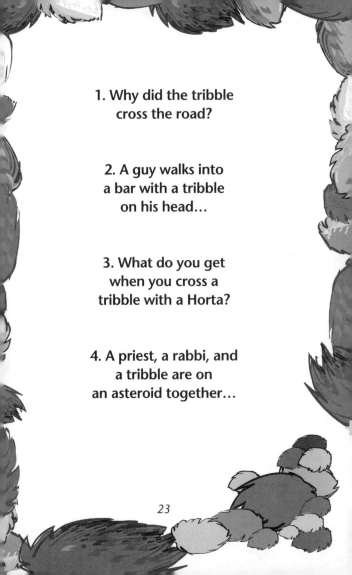

1. Why did the tribble
cross the road?

2. A guy walks into
a bar with a tribble
on his head...

3. What do you get
when you cross a
tribble with a Horta?

4. A priest, a rabbi, and
a tribble are on
an asteroid together...

23

5. Knock, knock…

6. There once was a
tribble from Nantucket…

7. How many tribbles
does it take
to fill the Albert Hall?

8. "That's not
my antenna."

9. What's the difference
between a tribble
and a moon rock?

10. Why did the Andorian
toss the tribble off
the Empire State Building?

11. How many tribbles
does it take to plug
in an isolinear chip?

12. Take my tribble—please!

WHAT BEC●MES A LEGEND M●ST?

A tribute. Or, rather, a tribblute.

The writers of *Deep Space Nine*, under the leadership of Executive Producer Ira Steven Behr, gave themselves a unique challenge: place the crew of DS9 into a storyline from the original *Star Trek*.

But which story?

They were inspired by one image— Captain Sisko, sitting inside the storage bin at Space Station K7, tossing tribbles onto Captain Kirk's head.

From there it was only a small step to imagining temperal investigators, predestination paradoxes and tribbles exploding in space.

And what better way to pay homage to the spirit of *Star Trek* than to seamlessly blend the old with the new, bridging the generations in high style and in the process, creating the brand new classic "Trials and Tribble-ations."

ENQUIRING MINDS WANT TO KNOW!

How Did the Tribble Cross the Road?

*A*ccording to Gary Monak, *Star Trek: Deep Space Nine*'s special-effects wizard, they did it the old-fashioned way.

"My main job on 'Trials and Tribble-ations' was to create movement for about seventy-five of the tribbles, but I had to do it in a way that matched the movement of the ones in the 1967

episode," says Monak. While technology has advanced a great deal in thirty years, sometimes the old ways are the best. "For the most part, they had done it by putting the tribble bodies on top of little windup toys," Monak relates. His crew also employed toys, but opted for battery-powered versions of such things as mechanical piggies, hopping penguins, remote-controlled motorcycles, and bubble balls with articulated motors that zigzag across the floor. Monak placed a radio-controlled servomotor inside the tribble that Odo introduced to Worf. "Whenever Rene Auberjonois held it up, we made it jump and jiggle," he says, laughing. And how did he direct the tribble to react so violently to *Star Trek*'s favorite Klingon? "With a joystick."

HOW DO YOU STUFF A WILD TRIBBLE?

Well, as you might expect, it involves some elective surgery—for both the tribble and its "donor." "We ran around for weeks buying toys and disassembling them," says Monak. "I felt like the mean kid in *Toy Story*—the one who was always tearing toys apart!" Once you have your mechanical guts, you open up a tribble's tummy (wherever that is), create a little pocket (don't worry, it probably doesn't hurt!) and insert your mechanism of choice. Only Arne Darvin and Gary Monak know for sure.